FIRST STORY
CHANGING LIVES THROUGH WRITING

First Story changes lives through writing.

There is dignity and power in telling our own story. We help disadvantaged young people find their voices.

First Story places professional writers into secondary schools serving low-income communities, where they work intensively with students and teachers to foster confidence, creativity and writing ability.

Our programmes expand young people's horizons and raise aspirations. Students gain vital skills that underpin their success in school and support their transition to further education and employment.

To find out more and get involved, go to
www.firststory.org.uk.

First Story is a registered charity number 1122939 and a private company limited by guarantee incorporated in England with number 06487410. First Story is a business name of First Story Limited.

First published 2019 by First Story Limited
Omnibus Business Centre, 39–41 North Road, London, N7 9DP

www.firststory.org.uk

ISBN 978-0-85748-357-7

1 3 5 7 9 10 8 6 4 2

A CIP catalogue record for this book is available from the British Library.

Printed and bound in the UK by Aquatint
Typeset by Avon DataSet Ltd
Copyedited by Olivia Kilmartin
Proofread by Beth Kruszynskyj
Cover designed by Sophie Thompson

I Don't Own the Alphabet, I'm Just Borrowing It

An Anthology by the First Story Group
at Addey and Stanhope School

EDITED BY ADAM Z. ROBINSON | 2019

FIRST STORY

CHANGING LIVES THROUGH WRITING

As Patron of First Story I am delighted that it continues to foster and inspire the creativity and talent of young people in secondary schools serving low-income communities.

I firmly believe that nurturing a passion for reading and writing is vital to the health of our country. I am therefore greatly encouraged to know that young people in this school – and across the country – have been meeting each week throughout the year in order to write together.

I send my warmest congratulations to everybody who is published in this anthology.

Camilla

HRH The Duchess of Cornwall

Contents

Introduction

Adam Z. Robinson, Writer-in-Residence

At the beginning of any course of writing workshops, you'll hear me say: 'In these sessions, it's impossible to be wrong. If it's creative and it's from you, it's right.' I was so impressed by how quickly my First Story group at Addey & Stanhope jumped into this idea and inhabited it. Their writing – as you'll see here in *I Don't Own the Alphabet, I'm Just Borrowing It* – is imaginative, bold and brilliantly playful. The stories and poems in these pages are fearless in their invention and delightful displays of the writers' immense creativity.

From the fantastic title (one from a list of many outstanding ideas, suggested and voted on by the group), to their answers to questions such as 'What's in the box?', 'What is home?', 'What's outside my window?' and 'What's through the keyhole?', the writers have demonstrated an outstanding ability to use, nurture and explore their own unique voices. Each piece in this anthology is different from the last, and any thematic similarities or shared titles are where the likenesses end. It was a privilege, week after week, to be dazzled and inspired by the originality each person brought to the table.

It was a pleasure, too, to be present for the beginnings of these ideas. Hearing the writers share their work is always my favourite part of the workshops, and seeing that writing collected here is a wonderful thing. I know you'll enjoy stepping into the worlds the writers have created. In 'You'll Never Believe This!', **Kaleib** introduces us to dapper skeletons and giant lizards, which may not be all they appear. In 'Cat-astrophe', **Marvin** brings us face to face with a dogged character's former feline foe. Astonishing fantasy tales are conjured in **Ryleigh's** 'Divine Intervention', **Jadon's** 'Monster of Garishef', **Oluwatomide's** 'The Power' and **Ruben's** 'Friend of Zarach'Zythe' where we get a glimpse of apocalyptic landscapes and thrilling, otherworldly characters.

We also have wonderful pieces that began life as entries to First Story's 100-Word Story competition: **Aishah's** devastating 'Drowning', **Aliya's** moving and unnerving 'The Fox' and **Milo's** fascinating, philosophical 'The Platypus'.

Janae presents us with an anxiety-laden everyday conundrum in 'Supermarket Dilemma' and in **Amina's** 'Sebastian Isn't Going Home' there's a powerful story about loss and being lost. In 'There Was a Man' by **Paddy**, and in **Wiam's** untitled story, there's a mounting sense of tension as the respective characters' true natures are revealed. Finally, **Obina** rounds off the collection perfectly by telling us, in his brilliant poem 'This Is What Home Means to Me'. These pieces truly are just the tip of the iceberg, too. Dive deeper and you'll discover the boundless fathoms of imagination of this extraordinary group.

Being a First Story Writer-in-Residence is a joy and a privilege. I have so enjoyed coming to Addey and Stanhope School each week and sharing the creative space with such exciting young minds. I'd like to say a big thank you to: the teachers, Daisy Mumba and Ebony Smith, who have been there each week and got stuck into the exercises themselves; librarian Kristabelle Williams, for inviting us into your wonderful space each week. Erika Gardiner, Head of English, for organising the First Story residency and a special thanks to Jan Shapiro, Head Teacher, for having us at Addey and Stanhope; Sophie Lloyd-Catchpole at First Story for her outstanding support throughout the programme; Jay Bhadricha, Gemma Harris and everyone involved in the editorial process. And finally, but perhaps most of all, to the writers! You've approached these sessions and writing tasks fearlessly and the fruits of your labours are here, in this wonderful book. I hope you will continue to write, explore and feel empowered by your voices.

And to you, reader: I hope you'll enjoy discovering the word-worlds that these writers have created for you. Enjoy the adventure. And remember – these writers don't own the alphabet, they're just borrowing it.

Teachers' Foreword

Daisy Mumba and Ebony Smith, Teachers of English

This is a collection of work by some truly talented writers. We are immensely proud of the progress made by each and every student who has contributed to this First Story anthology. Their unique contributions have allowed us to view the world through a multiplicity of lenses. We have been treated to glimpses of the surreal, the comic, the realistic, the gritty and the creepy. Our students have shown tremendous dedication to the programme, making us proud of their continued ambition and persistence to achieve excellence.

A special thanks to Adam Z. Robinson, without whom this would not have been possible. We are grateful to you for guiding the students through the creative writing process with such enthusiasm and sincerity. With your support, our students have been able to develop their artistic voice and communicate their unique perspectives on life. It has been a real delight to watch students expressing themselves in many forms and trying out a variety of new ideas.

Finally, a huge thank you to all at First Story for making this experience possible. We are delighted to have been part of such a worthy project, one that we believe has had a long-lasting and profound impact on our Addey's family.

I. Am. Freedom.

Oluwatomide Omojayogbe

Freedom has no home, he is always on the run.
Freedom runs from captivity,
Like a bird gliding from the cage.
Freedom loves all the animals of nature;
When he runs he thinks of running for change.
Freedom has a best friend called Joy.
Freedom has a problem:
Freedom has a lot of money;
Freedom is without bounds.
Freedom has a problem:
He has too much money;
What should Freedom do?
Freedom opens a bank account.
Now Freedom's only chains are clothes.

Destruction in Disguise

Amina Mohamed

The mirror saw everything. From the day it merged with the walls to the day it was shattered. It was useful in numerous ways: a plaything for a child trying to figure out how it worked; a way for the vain to admire their reflections; and − a witness. The frame of the mirror was inlaid with the most mesmerising carvings; it was the first thing that would captivate your eyes.

It was bought by a post-impressionist artist, who was fascinated by the frame's design and was inspired by the detail to finish off his painting. He named the painting after what he thought the carvings depicted, 'the starry night'. Sadly, a year later he committed suicide, without realising the mark he had made on the world.

A few decades later the mirror was passed along, like a burden nobody wanted. A burden that only shifted into its true potential in front of those who had the blessing of being able to spot the unordinary. Until, one day, the looking-glass was sold to a young lady who saw the same thing the artist saw: inspiration. Not to mention a good bargain as well.

She was an English lady who was charmed by politics and women's rights. Her heart was pure and righteous; she would often go to the mirror and encourage herself by saying things like 'no matter what they say, do not give in' or 'remember you are fighting for what is right; you are a suffragette'. She was a woman who always said she'd rather be a rebel than a slave.

Then on June 14, 1928, she died and her prized possession was given to the next-door neighbour's daughter. As a young child, she was particularly impressed by how large her reflection was when she first saw it. Each day her features grew more beautiful and elegant. Nothing and no one could compare to her. At least that's what everyone thought.

Her features were indeed attractive and her looks were flawless. But the mirror saw otherwise; what copied her reflection completely opposed her image.

On the other side, the mirror showed an uncanny figure trying to reach out as much as possible for an ounce of help. Each day its expression grew more exhausted than before.

One misty evening, a carriage parked itself outside the former suffragette's humble abode. The horses neighed and reared uncontrollably while the wind and rain combined to create a thunderstorm that would bombard the skies for the rest of the night.

Within the carriage were two gentlemen, unfazed by the sounds that shot across the skies. As they stepped out, both were greeted by a constable whose expression practically declared that he was in dire need of assistance.

He struggled to spit his words out st-stu- stutt-ering every second. 'P-please help before it... it... comes back to take the rest of us.'

The gentleman, who wore a deerstalker cap, fiddled around with his smoking pipe and held his magnifying glass in his other hand, unbothered by everything said to him. The other man, who stood next to him, clenched his briefcase and asked questions.

'What's going to get you?' he asked, intrigued, as he opened his notebook.

His whole body shaking, the policeman whispered all of the details, afraid that 'it' would hear him. 'Mr Holmes, help me destroy the mirror. My wife has gone but her body is still here. It may not make sense but I'll show you.'

First Day

Wiam Adeagbo

As the gate opened, she felt the warm breeze on her face. Her skin tickled from the drop of sweat that was running down her neck. Her dad was dragging a suitcase that contained her things. A man appeared from the corner. He seemed very short for his age. He was wearing a blue shirt and a pair of black trousers. He greeted her dad and nodded at her.

From the corner of her eye she saw a young, dark-haired girl peering and smiling at her from the window opposite. Her dad waved back.

She felt like crying. The short man took her to her room and everyone was looking at her. She felt anxious and started fiddling with the plastic ring that was on her finger.

That was her on her first day of school. That was Clarice.

What's in the Box?

Kaleib Belay

I strode towards the black leather box that stood ominously in the middle of the room, elevated by the equally black and equally leather pedestal.

The box opened with a creak to reveal another, slightly smaller, box... Weird.

Many hours passed of just box-opening. I was annoyed, but still excited by the prospect of what was definitively in the box, so I continued the tedious opening process.

I reached the end! I reached the end of this excruciating box nightmare and, savouring the moment, I opened the last box.

What was inside would shock a person with the strongest will, churn the stomach of the mightiest warrior and shatter the sanity of the greatest person.

Another box.

Criminal Crayons

Marvin Arthur

These illegal, vandalising weapons are wanted worldwide. The white-wall terrorisers travel in groups of fifteen criminal colours, consisting of the likes of Brooding Black, Rude Red and Beefy Blue. The ink of their former foes runs down the streets, striking fear into those who dare oppose them. Feared, revered and sharp on the rear, these graffiti goons terrorise the streets of Crayola.

From My Window

Ryleigh Williams

From my window I can see stars and stripes on a great blue flag,
waving at me through the wind, the sun rising over the horizon.

From my window I can see apartments for miles. Each lit up
by the glimmering ball of hope in the sky; it nearly makes
    me cry...

From my window I can smell the gas from vehicles
down below; the horns make a graceful sound.

From my window I touch the sunlight shining
over the top of the apartments, revealing the demons within...

From my window I can taste the despair of people suffering,
wandering into the dark unknown...

From my window I can see all my friends waiting for me.
This is my home, a vast unpredictable sea.

The Platypus

Milo March

Platypus sat at the end of the world, looking up at the midnight sky, watching the stars go dark. He wondered what it meant to be alive. *Was the idea of knowing you were going to die the thing that gave life meaning? Or was it the things one did in life that made it fulfilling?*

'I think I did things,' said Platypus out loud.

'You did alright,' a voice said from above.

'Did I though? What did I change?'

'Well, Emily wouldn't have found love, would she?' the voice said, amused.

Platypus started drifting upwards. 'True…'

What Do You Want?

Aliya Mans

I want it to rain;
I want to hear the sound of the rain pouring down,
as it bounces on the car, trying to find the right direction.

I want it to snow;
I want to see the crystal-white snowflakes pouring down
    the grey,
misty sky, as they change the concrete floor into a silky blanket
    of white.

I want it to be Friday;
not because I like it, but because it is closer to Saturday.

I want it to be summer;
I want to feel the warmth of the weather touching my
    sensitive skin,
like when I wore the orange flowery dress on my sister's
    birthday.

I want to be with my precious little puppies
because they know how to make me happy.

WHAT DO YOU WANT?

Me? I want to do everything, to do everything.
I want to be an actress, a judge, a singer, a lawyer,
and anything else the world has in store for me.

I want to change the world with my mind (not literally).
I want you to read this poem again.

The Phone

Janae Black

The door opened and Emily strode in briskly. It was the first day of her new, high-paying job. She was almost jumping for joy!

Before her, the grey room was separated into smaller sections, each of which was numbered one to forty-nine. They all contained a wooden table, a chair with wheels, a stack of paper and... an old telephone. None of these telephones worked anymore, but they stayed there because the manager wanted them for decoration.

Emily perched on the chair and grabbed some documents from her bag. She had to copy them by hand! She slowly reached for a sheet of paper and a black pen and began the painful process. It was surprisingly hard, and she constantly found herself making small mistakes, causing her to have to start again.

Then the phone rang. *Ring. Ring.*

Emily froze.

But how? Those phones don't work anymore! How could it actually be ringing?

What should she do? She was beginning to panic; what if this place was... *haunted*? She made a quick decision, one she would regret for the rest of her life.

She smashed the telephone to pieces on the chair.

Quite surprisingly, she was never allowed to return.

I Am

Jadon Black

I am freedom, hope and everything that comes with it.
I am the light-leading youth on a path of righteousness.
I am a mystery no detective can solve.
I am me, everything I want to be.

A New Perspective on Pet Shops

Jadon Black

I am looking through a keyhole. I can see a bald eagle with an aquiline shape. I can also see a snake slowly slithering on the ground, coiling around the class mascot: the soft tortoise. I also see a fat, green lizard banging at its cage door, hoping to escape its imprisonment.

Who Am I? An Awakening of a Human

Ruben Andre

I am a person who always acts shy.
I am a person who enjoys researching.
I am comprehensive in my stories.
I am looking for vocabulary that will help me in my GCSEs.
I am an all-knowing English child.
I am very careful with my words.
I am compelled to successfully succeed in my future assessments.
I am quite forgetful.
I am a special person.
I am never afraid of my mistakes.

I Come From

Ruben Andre

I come from trees, which give me pure life.
I come from a place where humans can say: 'Atmospheric'.
I come from a station staying idle for trains to stop and go.
I come from a workshop where mistakes don't exist.
I come from a game where technology is possible. *Press Start.*
I come from a YouTube channel where comedy and content
   exist. *MEME REVIEW!*
I come from a website, making tons of money. *Cha-CHING!*
   Money, money, moooney!

The Three 'Wise' Men

Paddy Jennings

In this box there is a dog. An English bulldog. He is an international business dog who has come to England to rob a bank. You might be thinking: *why would he need to do that? He is rich!* Well, that is a lie. He's broke! He spent *all* his money on dog toys, bones, dog nip, sticks and those cuddly rodents that squeak when you bite them.

So you see, he needs to rob the bank. Otherwise there'll be no more doggy biscuits for him! He is getting two of his best doggy friends to help him: Jim and Albert. His name is Ricky. Ricky the English bulldog.

Off go the three 'wise' dogs to rob from Her Majesty. They are not ready, not at all! But they still go to rob the bank. Apparently, this bank holds up to £1,000,000,000. That is enough to buy unlimited doggy treats! So they go to do the impossible heist.

They are all suited up. They have their balaclavas, their money bags, a map of the whole bank! The three 'wise' dogs walk up to the bank looking as cool as ever.

But... there is one problem. There is a cat. A bright ginger cat burglar that has messed up their whole dream.

Winter in a Nutshell

Obina Bromfield-Ehiwario

Through my window I can see the white shimmering snow
   falling outside.
Through my window I can smell hot chocolate and cinnamon
   as it swirls through the air.
Through my window I can hear the rain crystallise as it falls
   down from the white sky.
On my window I can touch the water as it trickles down
   my hand.
Through my window I can almost taste the snow as it melts
   in my hot and steamy breath.

Drowning

Aishah Taiwo

Drowning, that's the first thing I remember.

I remember the icy, blue, cold water grabbing my entire body, as if I was in court pleading 'not guilty' in front of the audience. Trying to catch my breath felt impossible. The taste of chlorine water rushing its way inside my mouth was unbelievable, not amazing, as it tasted like salt.

I could hear the voices of teenagers, toddlers and babies enjoying themselves while I was desperately calling for help, but no one answered. I remember seeing an army of waves crashing into me, as if I was driving a boat.

The Garden Falls

Milo Marsh

Uriel stood, head bowed, not affected by the wind whipping up snow. The huge golden gate hung in the air, a kilometre above the ground – a window to another world. Uriel held his sword. The tip of it stabbed into the frozen ground at his feet, and golden light shone from the cracks in the stone. Ornate carvings of branches wove their way up the blade, leading to a golden hilt that ended in roaring lion heads. The handle was made from an old, dark oak tree from deep within the garden. At the end of the hilt there was a white ball of marble held by claws.

Uriel had been tasked with guarding the Gates of Eden by God. He had stood at these gates since the humans had crawled out of the slime; none of them had discovered a way in yet. The Garden was a sacred place and only the humans who were willing could see it – willing to leave everything behind.

There were a lot of myths about the Garden. That humanity had started there. That Adam and Eve had been kicked out by God for eating an apple. Really, none of it was true. Uriel had found Adam bored one day and decided to let him see God's work. However, once Adam had been released into the world, Uriel had realised that Adam had been kept away from God's work for a reason. Adam was something of a god when released from his chains. He thought God's creatures weren't good enough. He had killed all of the others: *Homo erectus*, *Homo habilis*, *Homo floresiensis*, and all the rest of God's 'people'.

Uriel, seeing this, had engaged Adam in combat and cut him down, but not before Adam could forge a new race of his own in secret. It was made in his own image: the *Homo sapiens*. Uriel returned to God with Adam's body and God pulled out one of

Adam's ribs and created another being. He named her Eve, and she was tasked with overseeing the race Adam had created while God moved on to his next creations.

Uriel felt the air distort around him. Someone was here. He did not lift his head; he merely flexed his wings, sending out a pulse that stopped the current of wind. The snow died down and came to a rest around him. Whatever was coming was getting closer and was larger than any being Uriel had sent away before.

Uriel now stood in what seemed like an air pocket, with the blizzard outside still at full pelt. A silhouette appeared in the wall of wind and snow he had created. The figure got larger as it approached; it had grown beyond the size of a normal man now. Uriel lifted his head. *Leave now and forget.*

The figure stopped, reached into its pocket and withdrew a small object that was connected to its torso by a chain. Suddenly, Uriel flew back, hitting the wall of the mountain and sliding down it, dropping his sword. He saw that the man was dressed in a black waistcoat, the back of which was red velvet. The man had short brown hair swept up and back to the left with a streak of white at the front of his quiff. He clicked his watch shut and turned to the gate.

'The Garden of Eden, I've finally found you,' he said in a thick, exotic accent. He looked back at the angel, who was staggering to his feet.

Uriel picked up his sword and held it in front of him, bending his knees and putting his left shoulder forward. His red wings expanded, splitting in two.

The man cocked his head, 'What was that?'

Uriel lunged forward, swinging his sword at the man's head.

The man stepped backwards, bringing his left hand up to grab the side of Uriel's head.

A white light burst from his palm, shooting Uriel to the ground and skidding away.

The man turned back to the gate and walked forwards onto invisible stairs that led up to the gate. There was a resounding clang as the gates swung shut, and a rattle as a thick golden chain wrapped itself around the bars. A bright flash of golden light and the gate was locked.

Uriel stood, his sword pointed at the gate.

The man looked back and removed his pocket watch from his breast pocket. This time Uriel was ready. He threw himself to the right as a bubble of time froze in the area, just where he had been standing.

Uriel's wings beat and he flew into the air, hovering for a moment, and then came swooping down, swinging his sword as he did.

The sword caught the stranger's face and he fell from the steps, landing in the snow. Uriel circled above him in the air like a vulture and then came down on top of him, planting his sword in the man's shoulder.

Who are you? Uriel thought.

'Your salvation, my friend, and your damnation.' The man swung his legs, kicking Uriel's out from under him. The man stood, pulling the sword from his shoulder and brushing off the snow from his clothes, the scar in his face healing as he did. The man thrust Uriel's sword into his wing, pinning him to the ground.

'My name is Kronos, God of Time, King of Titans, and the Cleanser of Worlds. But right now, I'm the being who will destroy the Garden of Eden.'

He stepped over the struggling angel, a cylindrical device appearing in his hand. The device had two oval pieces of glass set in the middle, out of which shone a red and blue aura.

Kronos held up the device in both hands, and then twisted it so that the pieces of glass were aligned next to each other, releasing a beam of light that shot into the Gate. The golden chain cracked and white light shone from it, then it burst into a thousand shards. The Gates burst open and the warm air of the Garden blew out.

Uriel frantically tried to pull the sword from his wing but it would not move, as if it was being held there, frozen in time.

Kronos took his watch out of his breast pocket and opened it. He smiled and looked at the angel, angling the watch to face Uriel.

'And the clock stuck thirteen,' Kronos said. He turned back to the Garden. He then, with his left hand, tossed the device through the Gate into the Garden.

A lightning strike hit the area where Kronos stood and he vanished, as if he had never been there.

The sword finally slid from Uriel's wing. He staggered to his feet and moved towards the Gate. His wings combined once more and he lifted himself off the floor, desperate to retrieve the device.

A purple light burst from the Gate, sending Uriel flying backwards. The Gate convulsed and rippled in the air. Through the distortion, Uriel saw the garden burning in purple flame and the apple tree ablaze as a hundred voices cried out in fear.

The Gate disappeared, and Uriel was left hanging there in mid-air.

Through the Window

Oluwatomide Omojayogbe

Through the window, the wall lies.
Through the window, I look at the wall.
The wall is calling me, through the window.
They told me the wall was bad.
I wonder, through the window.
I want to know, through the window,
What is on the other side of the wall?
I feel drawn to the wall.
I wonder, through the window.

If I Were a Spirit

Jadon Black

Why must she haunt me so? Wherever I hide, she will never give up her pursuit. I feel her presence in my house, the smell of the gunpowder I used to smite her away. If only I were a spirit, I'd be free from the shackles that bind me to this torturous life. Stuck in a trench, within this psychological warfare, my tongue two inches too short to taste freedom.

'My life was never complete,' spoke the luminous beacon of white light. 'I have emerged from the shadows to explain to you what always seems to elude you. It's simple. You must sacrifice your soul to the Reaper, where you will finally rest... in...'

Tick Tock

Paddy Jennings

Tick tock. It struck twelve. *Tick tock.* It struck twelve. *Tick tock.* It struck twelve. It stopped.

Something was hiding in the clock. The glass smashed. A skeleton wearing clothes jumped out.

The story behind him is that he takes your skin and takes your identity. He commits crimes. Then he goes to his new victim… Oh yeah, did I mention he has been living in an old clock since 1781?

One day my friends and I were playing PS4. We heard someone outside the room. We didn't care. We carried on playing. Later on that night: *Bang! Bang!* It was coming from my clock! Nervously, I approached it. My friend joined me as I walked to the steamed-up, ancient clock… nothing.

The noise stopped. There was dead silence. I heard static – really loud static. It was coming from the living room. I was shaking out of my skin. My friend was nowhere to be found…

I was on my own.

A Day in the Life

Kaleib Belay

[START LOG]

Ahem, my name is War and, well… it's not going very well, but that's just how I like it. I've been given an interview sheet… not exactly sure how this works but let's go, I guess.

Where do you live?

That's a tricky question. You see, I don't live in one area. I'm what you would call nomadic. I travel wherever war and conflict is. I lived, a while back, in Europe, around 1914 or so, and now I live in Syria.

What hobbies do you have?

Oh! Yes, I have many hobbies, some of them being: war, of course; blood sports (when I lived with the Aztecs, I was hooked!); physical contact sports such as rugby; and weapons training. I mean, you can't be War and not know the ins-and-outs of weaponry.

Do you have any pets?

Pets? No, sadly. Due to how much I travel, it would be difficult to keep pets, but I have had my fair share of animal companions over many years. I had a horse companion called Betsie when I travelled with Genghis Khan, and a camel named Jamal when I fought during the Battle of Qarqar.

Do you have any enemies?

Of course I have enemies! I have fought in every single conflict throughout time! World War One, World War Two, the French Revolution, the American Civil War, the Mongol Conquests. But one enemy has stood out during the many years of conflict, one force that eventually drives me from war and to death.

Peace.

Mr Bigshot Peace waltzes in! 'No fighting' this and 'olive branch' that. It's absolutely disgusting – *honestly!* And you may be thinking: *great ol' War, why don't you just strike him down, like all of your other enemies?* But that's the thing, I can't. I've never been one to act inferior, but Peace is stronger than me… It doesn't matter if it's a scrap or a fully-fledged war, Peace always prevails in one way or another.

Peace always seems to straighten things out.

[END LOG]

Cat-astrophe

Marvin Arthur

Chicken and chips in hand, I approached my front door, only to be greeted by a former foe.

'Meow,' he purred, mocking my strength and courage.

I was angered by his smug remark.

'Ah my rival, you are a fool to step your filthy paws in my territory,' I proclaimed, still ten feet away.

'Meow!'

Seductive yet threatening meows bombarded my ears as I began to move closer. With all my courage building inside me, I unveiled my special attack:

'DAD! THE CAT'S BACK!'

I Want

Ryleigh Williams

I want to repair friendships
I want to relive old memories, good or bad
I want to say goodbye to all I have lost
I want peace and quiet
I want a house and a loud environment
I want my friends and family to prosper
I want someone to relate to
I want a planet to call my own
I want to revisit times with my father
I want adventure, to look at the open sea once more
I want to be me again

The Fox

Aliya Mans

As the predator crawled his way through the light, foggy forest, he already knew that someone or something was following him on the other side. He turned, urgently, to his left, wondering if he could sense anyone near him. Despite the fact that the Fox didn't have a name, he was still incredibly smart. His delicate, pointy ears heard a whisper behind him, saying: 'I am home.'

The small voice was recognisable, but it was hard to picture the speaker's face. The Fox stood up on his feet and started to pivot towards the stranger. And there she was…

Nooo! the Fox said to himself. It was just a dream.

The Fox ran home to his owner, Susan, to tell her his dream, so he could find an explanation for it.

Then, there was a loud knock on the door. *KNOCK-KNOCK.* Susan stood up and started to walk slowly towards the dusty window. She looked outside, desperately waiting for an answer, but she couldn't see a thing.

There was a knock again. It was much louder. Susan became extremely scared, but at the same time she was also angry. She approached the door with confidence and started to reach for the handle. The Fox started to follow her, as if he were her protector.

Susan suddenly opened the door – there was nothing. Susan and the Fox were confused. The Fox went slowly outside, but he couldn't see a thing. He could only see darkness.

He turned back around, so he could see his owner. Susan began to smile, from a distance. The Fox gradually walked closer, closer and closer. He thought to himself, *Why is she smiling?* But as soon he got near, he noticed that she wasn't smiling at all, but crying for help.

'Don't come any closer!' Susan exclaimed.

The Fox stopped, instantly. He started to walk backwards, slowly, as if she were attacking him.

As the Fox moved backwards, he felt something on his paw.

He felt that someone was behind him.

He turned and he saw… *her.*

Friend of Zarach'Zythe

Ruben Andre

As the sun rises and the birds chirp, a man whose name is Zarach'Zythe wakes up and eats breakfast. He is a thousand years old and lurks around sacred places. He watches the flowers bloom, happily, and he smiles.

'A beautiful day, as always,' he says.

As the day goes on, he walks outside his house for a breather. But before he can do anything at all, clouds cover the sky and something dark engulfs his home. He is scared, he doesn't know what is happening.

A black figure with red eyes comes running right at him, leaping towards him. But the figure stops and leans over.

It says: 'I am home, home at last. I can finally live with my family again.'

Zarach knows this voice but it is hard to see the face. The figure goes inside the house, into the kitchen, and turns on the light. Zarach follows.

It is HER, the one who abducted his family.

'ARGH! NOOOO!' exclaims Zarach in horror, then sighs in relief. 'Whew, was that a dream? I guess it was…'

He is still concerned about the legend of the person he saw in his dream. But either way, he doesn't want to think about it.

He hears a loud knock, and darkness engulfs the world. Zarach'Zythe, champion that he is, grabs a flashlight and opens the door. No one stands there, not a single figure.

Zarach is spooked, as many things might attack him. He slowly searches around the city, noticing screams every now and then.

I'm really scared, where is everyone? Why is there darkness? he thinks to himself.

Then he hears something that scars him for life: a painful scream, and a cry for help.

Zarach wants to help but he is too late. The screaming stops. He thinks they are dead... but no.

Zarach slowly walks backwards. He stumbles on a log, but continues to walk backwards.

He feels a light tap on his shoulder and he turns around, only to reveal: HER.

There is nothing but silence.

Sebastian Isn't Going Home

Amina Mohamed

As the bright candle in the sky dims, the moon rises from its slumber and a burst of luminous light jostles across the sky. Trees start to sway to the endless rhythm of the wind while the maroon-coloured leaves spiral into the mist of the night.

The weight on my shoulders is lifted and my face feels hydrated from the light breeze. If this is all just my imagination playing tricks on me, then I don't want to wake up. I can't tell if my eyes are open or closed, this must be my dream.

The palms of my hands are sweaty and my gut tells me to question everything, but at the back of my head I can hear a faint voice telling me not to worry. The tight knot in my stomach slowly unravels itself. Well, it won't hurt me to lie down for a bit. I stay on the grass and place my hands up high to feel the light breeze brush through the tiny hairs on my arms.

The radiance of the glowing sparks embedded in the sky captivates my eyes. I sigh and think about the life that's waiting for me when I wake up. Blank.

'Wait, where am I from again? What was I talking about?' I sit up cautiously, to take a look around. I'm alone. Why is no one here but me?

Clenching my fists, I struggle to remember where I'm from. My memories of my past feel like puzzle pieces pressed repeatedly into places they don't belong in. I can't think straight.

Then it happens.

The voice that reassured me, the voice that I thought was a beacon of safety is there, telling me not to be anxious. My throat dries up and the words I am struggling to say crumble to pieces. My face burns up and I break down, panicking.

I cry out loud: 'WHERE AM I? SOMEONE, ANYONE, TELL ME! Please.'

Then she speaks.

Her voice is so pure and elegant that it sends a soothing sensation through my body. Her words echo around my head and escort me to a tranquil forest that looks completely hidden from the outside world.

A jewel-blue stream ahead catches my attention. With each step I take, I think about the possibilities of where or what this stream could lead to. I think to myself for a moment: *Is someone waiting for me? Is it safe to go on?* My heart pounds twice as much as before and my hands feel like they've been drenched in water. Promptly walking along the stream, I pause and look at my reflection in the water.

A reflection of my past.

Gulping hard, I open my mouth and choke back the anxiety and tears that are flowing through my body.

Friendship Has a Life

Obina Bromfield-Ehiwario

Hello, I'm Friendship. I have a power. Do you want to know what it is... ? I can bring people together, like you, the readers, with my work of magic. I live in a world called Connected. My job is to make people become friends, no matter if they are enemies, because everyone can forgive. Hey, hello?

Hey you – HELLO... I'M TALKING TO YOU.

Can you look at me when I'm speaking?

Do I have to shout... ? Hey!

I've got a secret to tell you... Every time I get angry, I tend to break friendships and my anger can get the better of me sometimes. I can't control it and I don't know how to solve it.

Sometimes I feel corrupted, but I will never break your friendship, reader, don't worry. I'm here to help you, right? Sorry I went off-track there, the thought of getting corrupted permanently scares me. I have to go off and work now, I am needed somewhere out in this world called Connected. See you soon.

I Want to Go to the Moon

Janae Black

I want to go to the moon! But...

The moon is really far away. I would need *lots* of training to go there, because astronauts have to deal with a lack of oxygen.

My friend says it's easy, and it only takes a few weeks, and you would get used to not having much air. My friend also says that you will get very lonely if you travel to the moon.

I agree. What if you start to miss all the people back on earth? Well, to be honest, I don't think I would. But maybe I'd miss my family. My friend says there is only one solution to that – just get a cat and bring it with you into space!

What if the people (or creatures) on the moon speak a different language? How will I order food in a restaurant... or even know where the bathroom is? Am I supposed to carry my own toilet? My friend says you have to learn a language called Moonish... whatever *that* is.

Oh! By the way, my friend has never been to the moon!

What's in the Box?

Milo Marsh

What's in the box?
It's a cat,
No, it's a dog,
It's a hat,
No, it's a coat,
It's a pen,
No, it's a book,
It's a lake,
No, it's a hill,
It's a human,
No, I don't keep those,
It's a planet,
No, it's some sand,
It's a pie,
No, it's a cake,
It's a star,
No, it's cold,
It's a universe,
No, it's a cat,
It's a cat?
No.
Am I always wrong?

Chapter 1 – The Beginning

Aliya Mans

As the sun went down and the wind dropped, the woman was standing in the distance, waiting for an answer.

She walked tirelessly towards the young lad in the park, saying, 'Come with me.' But the boy, Alex, refused and started to run, as if someone was chasing after him.

A second woman, an older woman, walked swiftly towards Alex with open arms.

'Come with me instead and I will bring you home to your mama.'

He looked instantly to the old woman when she said that she would bring him back to his mother. Nevertheless, he still worried that she was lying. Then, it started to rain endlessly, in the middle of the night...

DRIP, DRIP, DRIP, DRIP, DRIP.

Alex started to wonder if he was in a long sleep, like Sleeping Beauty. However, he wasn't. It was real. The feeling of fear struck him as he was running towards an old, broken house. While he was running, he saw a shadow lurking behind him; slowly, slowly and slowly...

Then, he automatically stopped, without any warning. He could see the black showdown getting closer, closer and closer.

Monster of Garishef

Jadon Black

I am one who has no figure. A being who takes numerous forms. I will live on forever. And I have not lived at all. I am known as Death, the one who plucks out the souls of unresponsive bodies.

I wish to tell you of a hero who helped decrease my workload by a million. A brave and fearsome warrior. Her name was Madam McBufty.

In a small village called Garishef lived a massive, mucky monster. Blood spilled from its teeth as it devoured the two heroes of the village. Madam McBufty's closest friend was a sacrifice to fill its stomach. It spat out her bones, claiming they gave it gas. Madam McBufty escaped. But she was the only remaining survivor.

McBufty was special because she wielded the blade of disease and pestilence. She had to retreat, a strategic withdrawal. The monster was just way too powerful. She sprinted into the abyss of the woods, her only friend in this lonely world.

She poked herself with the sword and ran it along her skin. She dropped to sleep.

In her unconscious dreams she witnessed herself defeating the monster as her friends reappeared before her. She woke and forcefully bench-pressed her eyes open.

She saw me – Death. I transformed into a beacon of white shining light and spoke down to her.

'I have lent you my power so you can vanquish the evil monster known as BOBO. Use your power wisely.'

I left to scavenge a soul.

She ran back to Garishef, creating dust everywhere she

passed. She reached the town, which was now a shambles. She swarmed the lands, calling its name:

'BOBO! BOBO!'

She found it. She found the devil that had tormented her family. She used the power. A large explosion with a black flame. Dead.

To my surprise the monster dropped dead, too.

McBufty had made a noble sacrifice indeed. She had ended her life so she could kill the monster. Finally, I could take a well-deserved break. Sorry, a corpse is calling...

I Am

Oluwatomide Omojayogbe

I am so funny
I make extraterrestrials laugh in space
I am so wonderful
My wonder is uncontainable
I am so good
My goodness is contagious
I am so chatty
Aliens hear me on Mars
I am so in love with pizza
I could eat it three meals a day
I am so helpful
I can help three people at a time
I am so amazing
Stars follow me everywhere I go

Supermarket Dilemma

Janae Black

Kelly was standing in the canned-foods aisle in her local supermarket. She gripped two cans of beans in her shaking hands. Her eyes were darting between the cans and the credit card in her purse. She began to sweat. Her hands trembled as she put the beans in her trolley, and then she reached back in and took them out. The decision was almost overwhelming.

She hesitantly checked her credit card again, and then she gazed longingly at her favourite beans. Her problem seemed to be getting bigger... and bigger... and bigger! Her legs were so shaky that her knees were actually knocking together.

She couldn't take it anymore. Poor Kelly had to drop the beans and go straight to the till to purchase the rest of the food in the over-full trolley.

And she never got to have beans for her dinner.

You'll Never Believe This!

Kaleib Belay

'You'll never believe this,' was quickly becoming my most used phrase. I exclaimed it when that five-foot lizard climbed from my toilet and I shouted it when that skeleton jovially sauntered into my room, just to tip his bowler hat, wink at me, and leave.

My mum believes that I simply have an overactive imagination, but that doesn't explain the claw marks *on* and *in* the toilet, and the faint rattle of bones I hear each night.

It also, definitely, doesn't explain that one time when my light bulb decided, from nowhere, to sprout legs and jump from my window.

One day, the visions of dapperly dressed skeletons and disproportionally sized lizards stopped. They stopped when my mum came home from the doctor's. And with two pills and a glass of water, something happened…

It happened gradually, but over time the perceptions of the paranormal slowly started to fade. It began when the nightly occurrence of the skeleton was replaced by my dad simply wishing me goodnight. And then, the perception of the large lizard was restored to the sight of a spider, paddling pitifully within the bowl of the toilet.

My life used to be full of fun and mystery, but now it's comprised of encounters of the non-magical variety, such as going to school, eating food and… taking my pills.

The Root of Evil

Marvin Arthur

Evil is a crooked company-owner
profiting from the stupidity of his pathetic patrons.

Evil lives happily off peoples' failures in life, gaining fulfilment
from dragging others down to his level, which is considerably
low.

Evil eats lies like he does fries, with the side of tears as seasoning
each morning.

Evil's greatest wish is to deny everyone success while remaining
on top, with style of course.

But the one problem with Evil is Good.

From Evil's birth, Good has always been there to thwart his
schemes and claim all the fame while *he* is left to suffer. Because
Evil is alone.

And Evil is evil.

Divine Intervention

Ryleigh Williams

He failed…

Embers, death, and fire…

A man kneels, crying, holding the dead bodies of his wife and children.

'Who… who did this? Who killed them?' the man yells. His tears evaporate and fire is suddenly all around him.

Surrounded by ash and corpses, the man stands up and a dreadful silence sweeps across the land. A dark, twisted figure appears from the sky.

'Another mortal survived?'

Angry over his family's plight, the man burns the figure and it twists and distorts.

'YOU ARE NOT SAFE HERE, WORM…' and the figure fades into the sky.

The flames dissipate and the man falls down… unconscious. His name is Axis.

His city has evolved. The species – his species – has ascended to new heights.

The Cosmos in the Norm

Amina Mohamed

The man looked up at the moon and gave her a warm but sad smile. 'There's nothing wrong with hoping for it.'

In a bid to save his small yet comfortable planet, he called on the next one. In a gust of red dust and a hypersonic boom, a crimson shadow appeared before him. It stood still for a second and then condensed into a young boy, looking very annoyed, with his arms out, huffing and puffing. Mars had arrived. 'What is it that you want? Can't you see? I'm chasing the Martians off my planet!' he declared.

The Exotic Life of Failure

Amina Mohamed

Failure lives next door to Success. Only a few metres away.

Failure likes to regret the actions they've committed in the past instead of moving on.

Failure's best friend is Envy; it's a one-sided friendship where Envy is all Failure can think about.

Failure's job is to make sure no one gets near to Triumph.

Failure wears the clothes specifically chosen by Success to not stand out as much.

Failure's favourite thing to do is copy everyone else's moves and thoughts, so Failure can blend in.

Failure wakes up in the morning and sighs and reminisces about every mistake made by Humanity.

Failure knows everybody and everybody is familiar with Failure.

Failure is avoided by everyone.

But if Failure didn't exist, Success wouldn't either.

The Power

Oluwatomide Omojayogbe

There was a boy called John. He was an amazing swimmer and loved to try new things if he could. But he had a problem. He would hear voices in his head telling him to do things that would help him do the right thing; it was as if he had a guardian angel. His life changed when he went on a school trip to the museum.

In the museum, there were many fantastic and beautiful things! John got separated from his group. He had felt weird since entering that place of history.

He found a key, in a secret room. The key was calling to him; it was like he was at one with it, like the key was connected to his spirit. As he picked up the moulded gold object, a door appeared. John used the key to unlock the door; he walked through it with wonder.

When he entered this mysterious space, a being of light with beautiful, white wings appeared. John realised that this was his guardian angel.

The angel spoke and said: 'John, *you* are an angel too. One that could kill the devil.'

John knew from this day forward his life would never be the same. He would have a whole new responsibility.

Ghouls 'n' Ghost

Marvin Arthur

The door had been nailed shut for no reason, as if it was another cruel prank by my siblings.

'But they are still at school,' I thought aloud.

Suddenly there was a crack, a slam and a whoosh, a bright light. I rushed towards it. Only the closer I got, the more the light faded and its true form became apparent. I tried to stop but at this point I was too close to turn back, and before I could even process this, it went black.

'This is it,' I murmured to myself.

Lights flickered and machines of some sort blasted a cheerful tune and I heard a voice in the distance.

'All aboard and get ready for the time of your life,' the ghastly ghost announced. 'Welcome to the Ghouls 'n' Ghost Railway!'

Shocked and confused, I contemplated my options, but curiosity got the better of me and I ran to the conductor-suited ghost. He greeted me.

'Welcome aboard m'boy!' he wailed. 'All aboard the ghost train.'

'Where?' I questioned.

'Right here!'

Suddenly, as if I was blindfolded for the whole experience, a train filled with ghouls and ghosts arrived. I managed to find a seat next to a window, between a friendly-ish looking ghoul and what appeared to be his dog.

The train started to move.

'When is the next stop?' I yawned to the ghoul.

'Next stop?' he repeated back to me, looking confused. 'This is our life now! For the train is life and we are aboard till the end of time.'

'Maybe I should just rest. I'm probably just seeing things.'

I woke up feeling a lot lighter than before, like a feather in the wind. But for some reason, I was still in the clanky contraption.

I stood up.

'Where's the toilet?' I asked the ghoul.

'It's to the left, down the hall,' he groaned back to me.

I put my hand on the door handle and, to my surprise, I flew through it. I dashed to the sink to wash my face. It felt like days had gone by here. Shocked, surprised, startled: these were the emotions I felt when I looked in the mirror. Why? I was transparent with a strong cartoon outline. I looked to my hands, my fingers turning to nubs. I looked at my feet, coiling upwards, and I looked in the mirror once again, and I was a ghouls'n'ghost.

The Cold

Milo Marsh

The night was unforgiving; the trees had been swallowed from her sight. Mrs Anderson stood at the window of the wood cabin, her breath becoming mist on the glass.

The orange glow of the fire danced on the walls and the side of her stony face. A log on the fire crumbled. Snow drummed on the windows like the tapping of fingers. The night was black and Mrs Anderson could see her white face reflected, frightened, in the glass. She placed her hand on the transparent barrier, feeling the cold bite her skin. Her hands appeared slender in the reflection, slender and cold.

The cabin was an old one, built by her great grandfather. It was made from pine trees (and was their tombstone). A cobblestone fireplace jutted out from the east side of the building, stretching up, but dwarfed by the surrounding trees.

She heard a shuffle from outside.

She looked towards the door, the two bolts still in place, holding it firmly shut. It was getting closer.

She turned back to look out of the window to see what was causing the noise – perhaps a lost fawn.

She looked back outside, her heart racing.

A grinning face stared back at her and the slender hand, on the other side of the glass, closed its icy fingers.

Homeless in the Snow

Jadon Black

I enter the war zone.
I hear the boots crunching in the snow.
I see the white duvet covering the slate roofs.
I smell the hot chocolate in the shop, forever longing for a sip.
I feel the snow biting my ears, making me shiver.
I taste the cold reality of having no home, not even Crisis
   at Christmas.

What Would You Expect?

Aliya Mans

As the clock struck ten, I already knew that I was supposed to be awake. I heard the sounds of birds chirping sweetly outside my window, while the burning-hot sun was getting into position. The glimmering light scattered in all directions in my room before it found its way onto my upper eyelids, which is the most delicate part of your eye skin.

My eyes opened swiftly and gently, one by one, as if I was opening them for the first time.

'ANDREW, COME DOWN THIS INSTANT!' yelled David, my step-father.

'WHY? HAVE I DONE SOMETHING TO UPSET YOU?!' I said, with no remorse.

Then David's voice got angrier, 'DON'T MAKE ME REPEAT MYSELF!'

'Okay, okay, I'm coming,' I said, while I was trying to get up from my cosy bed.

Before I was rudely interrupted by my no-good step-father, I had meant to introduce myself.

My name is Andrew. Andrew Frankston. The son of Patricia Frankston and Phillip Frankston.

However, my father died in a car crash on my birthday, which makes him the most important person in my life.

And then you meet David. David, David, David. Where can I start? A man who loves hanging out with his friends, rather than hanging out with his family. A man who enjoys partying every night, without telling my mum. And he doesn't even like me.

I Know

Janae Black

I know that the beginning is always the end.
I know that stories are written in books.
I know that the Earth is my home.
I know that nothing is something.
I know that light is the window to my soul.
I know that space is just a metaphor for emptiness.
I know that the end is always the beginning.

I Am

Janae Black

I am that mouse creeping around behind the walls,
the one you can never find.
I am that fish, the one you can never hear,
but always the most observant.
I am that spider lurking under your bed,
the one you can never see, but always know is there.
I am that cat, dashing from place to place,
the one leaving too quickly to make their presence felt.

The Myth that Haunted All Races Worldwide

Ruben Andre

Five hundred thousand years ago, a myth, argued by many, emerged from among the human race. It is told that a mysterious box was known to be sealed shut and haunted those who approached it. The story of the box is the oldest, most terrifying story of them all. And now it's your turn to listen to this forbidden tale.

The year was 2001. I was all alone, just an average, normal person, wandering around restricted places. No one needs to know how I got past those rotten graveyards and through those broken walls. All we need to know is it was time to find this sacred box, located at the abandoned mansion.

This box was known to give many – and I mean *many* – gifts and treats. But why were people afraid of it? Perhaps it was the excessive opening of it. I walked to where I predicted the box would be. Apparently, it was five miles away. So, I walked for about five hours. After those said hours, I reached the mansion, at long last. It was there, right in front of my eyes. With great might and bravery, I entered the mansion. But... and this is a big but... my heart stopped. Like everything was ending. I realised I had made a grave mistake. I realised that death would meet me, every step of the way...

Wind blew through my hair. I walked up the dead, horrific steps of the entrance of the mansion. I couldn't stand the ghoulish noises that I heard on occasions. I explored the abandoned mansion, with fear dragging me down like a fifty-ton anvil. I looked in the fridge to find something to eat, but the rotten smell of meat and milk gave me a nauseous pain for a few minutes. By 'a few minutes' I mean fifteen minutes flat. I had to explore the mansion while vomiting every second. So, next I checked in the kitchen; no box yet. The kitchen looked clean but all of the dishes looked rusty. I checked for some stuff to loot: nothing good but a key. *What would a key do here?* I thought to myself. But I moved on regardless.

Introducing: The Living Room. Good ol' living room I must say, but now that I think about it… the couch covers, the smell of rust and gross drunk vomit. Consequently, I had another nauseous pain for an extra fifteen minutes. But I had no time to worry about it. I needed to check the other parts of this wretched mansion. I vomited as I leaned over to the couch. After a few examinations and investigations, it was finally time to find this box. I looked to see if there was a locked door. It wasn't easy.

The locked part of the mansion? You guessed it, the basement. Classic spooky reveal. So, I put the key inside the keyhole and turned it slowly, at the same time realising this was my final step to finding out if this box was a myth or an actual object. This was it, the final showdown. With great bravery and putting on the stance of a fighter, I drop-kicked the basement door and charged into the darkness, only to fall unconscious after running into something strange… was it a wall? I was utterly confused and surprised at the same time. So, all of this fear I had to go through was but wind and air? Without a single word of response, I ran away in dismay and anger. I never should've gone on that stupid quest. I came home, and collapsed in relief afterwards, never to fall for something like that again…

2051. A scientist called Depth Calibur concluded that the myth of the mysterious box is, indeed, real. Many people say it is fake, those dead-minded people, not learning anything after these eternities. Calibur discovered, also, that the box was last seen in an abandoned mansion. People argue that there was no such thing as a stupid mansion that was abandoned by a dead family, or something along those lines. But Calibur was not wrong, he had evidence. The evidence to show everyone its identification. And so it begins once again. The box was real the whole time. No one has found it, and now they will feel pain and distress again.

There Was a Man

Paddy Jennings

There was a man. He was unknown. No one knew his name. *Did he even have one?* I asked myself.

I had been tracking him down for two years until I eventually found him; I learnt only one thing. He despised crime. He would force himself to go to court every day to leer at the monsters, waiting for them to be prosecuted.

I realised something about his past. His mum and dad were both killed and the people got away. That must hurt.

A month later, and I have learned his name. Alfie. And he is an army reject. I have watched him quietly for years. I live in his house, I live inside the cracks of his walls.

I watch him sleep. Well, when he does sleep, which he rarely does. But now the secret has been revealed: he's after me.

I am the man with blood on my hands.

I had been led to think that he was just a normal man. Oh well. Will get him next time.

What's in the Box?

Obina Bromfield-Ehiwario

The word 'box' could be a portal to another dimension, watching what I was doing ten minutes ago. To be honest, I don't know what is in the box. I have been told to 'use my imagination' and I can't use anything in my brain. I wish I knew what was in the box, but that would defeat the purpose of the surprise. I just see a rugged black box with what might be just books inside or maybe just nothing. All I can think of is the word 'box', but not what's inside the box. I'm just going to guess that I'm not supposed to guess what's in the box.

Hearts, Knives and a Box

Amina Mohamed

Inside the box lies humanity's deepest darkest secrets – a reflection of mankind's true nature, kept hidden by leaders of the world – piling up over millions of years.

The leaders' aim is to keep the abyss of treachery and shameless actions undiscovered by all.

The box gobbles up all sins and actions. One day it will self-destruct and finally be obliterated, but when it does, we perish too.

However, of course, the leaders of today have also selfishly discovered a way to keep themselves and a few others alive and well away from sin.

A selection. A roll of a dice.

Like *The Hunger Games* but without tournaments, hunger, romance, and most of all a happy ending.

The overly confident and most absurd warriors are chosen by the infected nations, to be then booted off into the crate of death.

The soldiers are influenced and trained to think that once they leap inside those boxes, their anxieties shall disappear.

And technically it's the truth, since you can't feel worried when you're dead.

So let us begin the game of your demise.

Untitled

Wiam Adeagbo

23rd March was the date I moved to Kent.

I packed my belongings and went in the car alone. It was freezing so I decided to turn on the heater. Then I remembered that I hadn't bought the gas for the heating. I put on my coat and scarf, and I set off.

It's gonna be a long day, I thought.

One hour later
I was at Dartford. I stopped at a nearby cafe to get some coffee. As I stepped into the cafe, I felt the warmth of the room. All the seats were occupied except one. So I decided to give my order and head to a seat. In front of me was a young man who was wearing all-black clothing, including dark shades (in winter). He was looking down at his coffee. Suddenly, he looked up and our eyes flickered. I got really scared and walked quickly out of the cafe.

As I was about to continue my journey, I looked behind me and I saw the strange-looking man was about to get into his car. Then I started to drive as quickly as possible.

Thirty minutes later
I didn't know where I was; I thought I was lost – until... I spotted a car behind me, driving really fast.

Five minutes later
I got anxious because the car was moving really fast. It was close to me. I decided to turn left, but the car followed me. I noticed

in my rear mirror that the person driving the car was the young man I had seen at the cafe.

He had been following me all along. Then suddenly I stopped.

The man stepped down from his car with a coffee in his hand.

'I just wanted to give you back your coffee; you left before your order came... Why were you in such a hurry?' the man said.

Looking through a Keyhole

Kaleib Belay

The keyhole stands there, mocking me, shielding my vision from the terrors that lie outside the door.

He's been there for a while now; he refuses my cries and yells to leave. A terrible grin engulfs his face; he knows the utter torment he is causing. He revels in the pain that I feel at this very moment.

'Please leave.'

Wham's Wish

Marvin Arthur

Wham the Wizard promised us one thing and that was a wish. Little did we know, any wish would come with a price that we would have to pay.

Oh, what did yours cost you? you might be thinking. Well, it cost me an arm, because what I wished for was beyond even Wham's grasp.

What did you wish for – to lose an arm? you might also be thinking.

Pizza. I wished for pizza.

Tell Me What You Know

Aliya Mans

I know that I have a phone right with me
I know that I'm wearing some shoes
Obviously, I know where I live
I know that we have eight fingers, not ten
I know that some people enjoy waking up early and some
    people don't
I know that after autumn is winter
I know how to count to ten, surprisingly
I know how to spell my name: A-L-I-Y-A
I know how to ace anyone in a game
I know my mum's phone number, but I don't know my own
I clearly know my left from right
I know how to speak and understand French
I know how to access the Internet without using my phone
And I know how to be myself

I Know

Ryleigh Williams

I know that I have two homes.
I know I have people who care.
I know that this world is boring.
I know that life is great.
I know that, as my mother's son, I'm the one and only.
I know that I know that I know a lot of stuff.
I know a lot of dumb things.
I know I'm in a book.
I know that you know that you don't know who I am.
Until now.

Beehave

Jadon Black

From my window this is what I saw:
Sitting on the brick wall
a big yellow bumblebee.
So I decided to visit the mall.

I had to collect bug spray.
But in a hurry, I lacked money.
So I carved fake cash out of clay.
And I stole repellent and ran away.

In a big hurry, I heard a loud noise.
It was the cops.
I realised that I needed some decoys.
I needed to hop.

In my escape, the bee stung me.
Police caught up and I got captured.
So in my prison window was a dead bee.
And my skin was fractured.

Kindness

Milo Marsh

Kindness is a four-year-old who is happily unemployed.
Kindness walks around town and often meets new people, says
    'hi' and then carries on walking.
Kindness hangs out with its friend Peace; they get on really
    well.
Kindness likes to wear bright colours and large Hawaiian
    shirts.
But sometimes Kindness gets shy and doesn't come out and
    Peace is left all alone.
Peace can't always get back because of the people that push
    past her on their way to nowhere.
They ignore the kid crying,
The kid crying and screaming until her eyes are red.
No one cares that she's alone,
They don't know why she is not happy.
They just hate her for it.
They sometimes kick her and make her move out of their way.
She cries for them to stop,
But they never do.
They carry on, relentless,
But when Kindness comes she cheers up.
Kindness comes and picks Peace up and walks her through the
    crowd.
Peace smiles and wipes her eyes.
And the crying stops and people relax.
They smile.
And Kindness walks the street with Peace under its arm.

The Mirror

Wiam Adeagbo

I woke up in the middle of the night from the loud howling of my dog. I was about to stand up from my bed when I felt a sharp pain in my right eye. Then I glanced at the mirror. I can barely describe what I saw.

I saw something behind me. I turned back to see what it was. But it was gone. I only felt a gush of air on my face.

Then I looked back at the mirror. The strange-looking thing was still staring and moving behind me. I looked back again, but it was still gone. Then I tried the most ridiculous thing ever. I touched the mirror and I got sucked in.

This Is What Home Means to Me

Obina Bromfield-Ehiwario

It is the place that keeps me safe at night
It is the place that looks after me
It is my one and only best friend
It is my vacation on a secret island
It is the foundation of my family's most treasured memories
It is what I grew up in
It is the most clean house
It is what I call home

Six-Word Biographies

Wiam Adeagbo: Make a mistake. Learn from it.

Ruben Andre: I am reborn. Showered in light.

Marvin Arthur: Rule breaker. (It's not six words.)

Kaleib Belay: Amazing person. Also, a compulsive liar.

Jadon Black: A young child with crazy ambition.

Janae Black: A quiet girl that eats pie.

Obina Bromfield-Ehiwario: Gaming's my life. Singing's my talent.

Paddy Jennings: Don't give up. That's not right.

Aliya Mans: 'Just get on with it.' (Waiting.)

Milo Marsh: Six-word stories are for nerds.

Amina Mohamed: Brexit being delayed is the best.

Oluwatomide Omojayogbe: Games. Fun. First Story joyful writer.

Aishah Taiwo: Annoying, funny, strong-minded, loves spicy food.

Ryleigh Williams: 'Ryleigh!?' Oh… I don't see him.

Acknowledgements

Melanie Curtis at Avon DataSet for her overwhelming support for First Story and for giving her time in typesetting this anthology.

Olivia Kilmartin for copy-editing this anthology and supporting the project.

Sophie Thompson for designing the cover of this anthology.

Tony Lyons and Kate McLean at Canterbury Christ Church University for their support.

David Greenwood and Foysal Ali at Aquatint for printing this anthology at a discounted rate.

HRH The Duchess of Cornwall, Patron of First Story.

The Trustees of First Story:
Ed Baden-Powell, Aziz Bawany, Aslan Byrne, William Fiennes, Sophie Harrison, Sue Horner, Sarah Marshall, Betsy Tobin, Jamie Waldegrave, Katie Waldegrave.

Thanks to:
Arts Council England, Alice Jolly & Stephen Kinsella, Andrea Minton Beddoes & Simon Gray, The Arvon Foundation, BBC Children in Need, Beth & Michele Colocci, Blackwells, Boots Charitable Trust, Brunswick, Charlotte Hogg, Cheltenham Festivals, Clifford Chance, Dulverton Trust, Edith Murphy Foundation, First Editions Club Members, First Story Events Committee, Frontier Economics, Give A Book, Ink@84, Ivana Catovic of Modern Logophilia, Jane & Peter Aitken, John Lyon's Charity, John Thaw Foundation, Miles Trust for the Putney & Roehampton Community, Old Possum's Practical Trust, Open Gate Trust, Oxford University Press, Psycle Interactive, Royal Society of Literature, Sigrid Rausing Trust, The Stonegarth Fund, Teach First, Tim Bevan & Amy Gadney, Walcot Foundation,

Whitaker Charitable Trust, William Shelton Education Charity, XL Catlin, our group of regular donors, and all those donors who have chosen to remain anonymous.

Most importantly we would like to thank the students, teachers and writers who have worked so hard to make First Story a success this year, as well as the many individuals and organisations (including those who we may have omitted to name) who have given their generous time, support and advice.